WYND™

BOOK ONE: THE FLIGHT OF THE PRINCE

Published by
BOOM! BOX™

BOOM! BOX™

WYND Book One: The Flight of the Prince, May 2021. Published by BOOM! Box, a division of Boom Entertainment, Inc.

BOOM! Studios, 5670 Wilshire Boulevard, Suite 400, Los Angeles, CA 90036-5679. Printed in China. First Printing.

ISBN: 978-1-68415-632-0, eISBN: 978-1-64668-044-3

Limited Edition
ISBN: 978-1-68415-709-9 , eISBN: 978-1-64668-253-9

WRITTEN BY
JAMES TYNION IV

ILLUSTRATED BY
MICHAEL DIALYNAS

LETTERED BY
ADITYA BIDIKAR

COVERS BY
MICHAEL DIALYNAS

CREATED BY
JAMES TYNION IV
+ MICHAEL DIALYNAS

PROLOGUE
THE NIGHTMARE

mm

mmnnn

Nn

Nnn--

NO!
WHAT.
N?
AARG
SKRRR

KKKKKKK
FT
Wynd? Are you there? I heard a noise...

W-Wynd?

What did you do to him?
WHAT DID YOU DO?!
FTANG
FTAK
FTAK

FTAK
FTK
DAK
FTAK
DUP

WYND

BOOK ONE:
THE FLIGHT OF THE PRINCE

BY **JAMES TYNION IV + MICHAEL DIALYNAS**
WITH **ADITYA BIDIKAR**

CHAPTER ONE
THE DARK SPOUT

Hah, I *knew* it!

You slept in again!
Whuh...
You missed the *morning bell.* C'mon, you need to get dressed!

Get... dressed?

Oh. Okay.

Keep this up and Mom is going to come down here and serve *you* for breakfast.
I'm moving!

Look. I'm not going to leave for the day shift until you at *least* have pants on. Imagine if the entire waste system of *Pipetown* backs up.
All over a pair of pants.

I'm putting them on!

Okay, it's time to wake up for real.
LIVE
THE DARK SPOUT
I'm awake. Just had...a weird dream, is all.
Just trying to get my head straight.

That's your excuse every morning.
What do you even dream about?
YAWN!

Bad stuff, Oakley. Let's drop it, okay?
Like you said. Time to get to work.

I just wish you could come to work with me. I don't like leaving you here alone each day.
LIVE THE DARK SPOUT
I don't want to be a part of the Engineering Corps.
I like smelling like *food,* not sewers.
You smell more like *grease,* but okay.

I *like* it here. I like *working* here. And I'm going to be here at the end of the day, like I always am.
I'm good, Oakley. I promise.

Your shirt's on backwards.
Maybe I *like* my shirt on backwards! Maybe it is my cool new look.
You're such a dork.

Make sure to keep these covered, 'kay?
I like Titus a bunch, but he's still new and he might not understand. Got it?
Yeah, I know.

Bye,
Oakley!
BYE!!

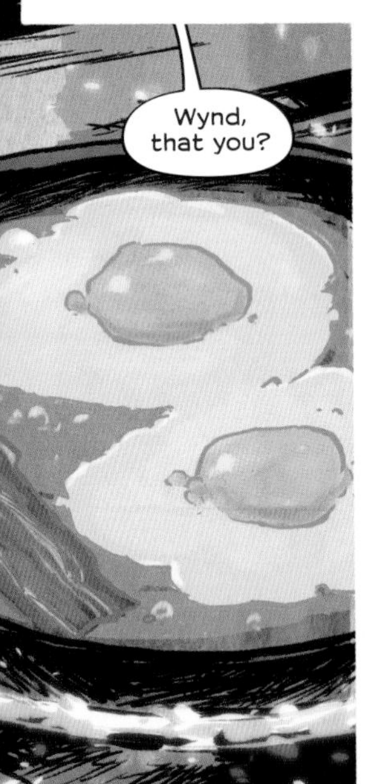
Wynd,
that you?

It's me,
Titus!
First orders
coming up in
a minute.
Standing by!

Is that boy awake yet?
I swear the entire
Engineering Corps decided
to stop in for coffee and
bacon this morning.
I'm awake,
Miss Molly.

You know,
if you woke up
a little earlier
you'd be able to
take a ***shower.***
Wash that
unruly hair
of yours...

I'll do all that later.
Oh, child. Don't lie to me.
Okay.
Table Fourteen is up!
Four, Six, and Twelve coming in fast behind them!
DING!

I have to get back up there or they'll start pouring for them-selves.

Got it!

SLAM
TURN

FDING!
FWOOSH!

FWOOSH

FDING!

FWOOSH

FDING!

Y'know. I saw him the other day, walkin' in to the castle gates.
A real look of *menace* to him.

What nonsense is this now, Henry?

The King's called back the *Bandaged Man* from Northport.
Brought 'im in to help weed out the *Weirdbloods.*

Don't know where he expects to find any. I remember the cullings when I was in the Corps.
The floodgates have stayed shut for a generation.

Only *pointy ear* I've seen is Patrick's, and that's 'cause he nicked it once with a bad haircut.

Hic!

You know some of the trade gates are sloppier than others. You know there's folk against the *Blood Laws.*
You're too smart, Molly. Too smart to pay them much mind. But we all know there's *weird* ones walking among us.

Ones with a bit of *magic* to 'em. Not so much they can't hide it, but enough to infect the rest of us if they get out of hand.

We gotta be more vigilant. It's ***good*** the King brought the Bandaged Man back to Pipetown.
Hopefully it keeps the lot of them scared out of here.

You talk too much, Henry. And that hair of the dog is getting a little too hairy, if you ask me.

You should get home. Night shift will be back 'round before you know it. Get some sleep.
SPLSH

Aye... I should.

Just keep your eyes open, Molly. If the King is worried that something is afoot in Pipetown, we should be worried, too.
Keep the ones you trust close, and keep your eyes on everyone else.

I will, Henry.

I'm heading down to get another barrel. You lot need anything?

I need a barrel of purdy golden eggs.
I think we're fresh out, Patrick, but I'll check for ya.

AP
TAP
TAP
TAP

Wynd?

Everything alright, Miss Molly? You have a look about you.
It's fine, Titus. Every-thing is fine. Where's the boy?

He took off after the morning rush, like he always does. He's always back around **noon** before folks come by for lunch. Always **blushing.**
Think he's got an eye on someone out there, Miss Molly. I keep trying to get it outta him, but he keeps his lips shut.

He in trouble? Is that it?
He's not in trouble.
Okay.
Seriously, Molly...What are you worried about?

Never you mind, Titus.
Never you mind.

HERB's GREEN

PIE
HAPPY HOUR

Okay...
I know you're out there.
You're not going to skip a nice morning walk on a day like this?
No, of course you aren't.
KLK!

"Why, hello, Wynd. It's good to see you again! How was the morning rush?"
I barely screwed up any plates this time, Mister Gardener. Everyone got their breakfasts.
"Oh, I bet you haven't screwed up in months, and you're just being modest."
Why don't you come by for dinner, and maybe I can show--
The Bandaged Man...
...

GULP

CHAPTER TWO
WEIRD BLOOD

Ey, Pop? You in here?
Aye, son. I'm here.
The Bandaged Man stopped me on my morning run...
Didn't know he was going to be coming back to the castle.
Yes, yes. Very good.
No, Dad. His *voice* makes my skin crawl. You know that.
Hmm.

You're not listening to me.
No, boy. I'm not acknowledging you. There's a difference.

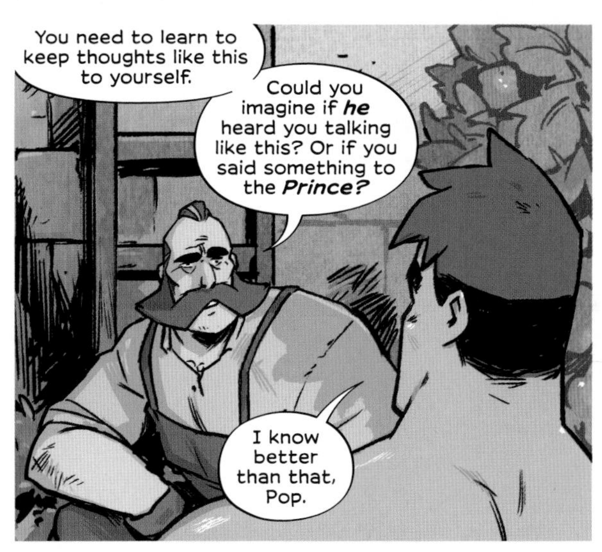
You need to learn to keep thoughts like this to yourself.
Could you imagine if he heard you talking like this? Or if you said something to the Prince?
I know better than that, Pop.

Good.
What are you looking at?

This back bush in the greenhouse here. It's been allowed to grow wild. Hasn't been a wild bush in Pipetown in a century.
If the King found out, he'd have my skin. It's been our family's job for generations to keep the greenery properly tamed.
To keep the Sprytles out.

Sprytles?
See it there? Small. Just a babe.

GAH

Don't let it touch you. It has an ***innocent*** nature, but should it take hold of you, it'd ***twist*** the blood running through your veins.
Taint you with its ***weirdness.*** Its ***wildness.***

Its ***magic.***

GEEEBO!
Awww...

Fawn all you'd like, Thorn. These damned things ran our ancestors out of the *Boreal Waste,* and the *Notunlands.*
They're the reason Pipetown is the last pure human stronghold in the damn world.
No matter what those *Weirdbloods* in Northport would have you think.

You haven't seen them, boy. The people twisted up into wretched beasts. Their *skin* turned to *bark.*
SNP

Branches coming out of their *eyes.* Their *tongues* sprouting *flowers.*
SNP
SNP

The world is *wild,* and we mustn't forget it. Men like the Bandaged Man, they keep the streets *safe...*
SNP
SNP
SNP

G-geebo...

SHNK
It'll be your job one day to keep these grounds. To maintain this garden. You'll be the one holding back this ***chaos.***
Yes, Father.

Young Master Cherrywood.
Heya, Basil.
Prince Yorik requests your presence in his quarters.
Yeah, okay.

Maybe a ***shirt*** first, boy.
What?

Oh.

All well here, Ash? Nothing ***weird?***
Fine, Basil. All fine.

I think Thorn can find his way up on his own. Been walking these grounds longer than he's been talking.
Perhaps a bit ***too*** freely.

You're the one bringing him to the Prince's chambers. Not me. I won't have you giving me guff about our family's place.

That's not--
No matter.

Tell the boy I'll meet him in the ***entrance hall.*** Security in the castle is getting more rigid.
Aye.

Pop...
Be careful.

I know.

No, you ***don't.*** You're blinded by youth and loyalty and everything a boy your age should feel.
And maybe a little bit ***more*** than that.
Daaad...

But a decade on, he'll be on that ***throne*** and you'll still be in these ***gardens.***
Don't forget that.

I won't, Pop.

It's so quiet in here.
Yes...Given the King's *illness,* it's been determined that the *court* stay out of the castle.
I must admit, I miss the *music...*
Wait here a moment, I'll announce you to the Prince.

Yeah. Okay.

This way, Thorn.
Yeah... Of course.

You came.
Yeah.

You have come to my *Den of Misery.*

So, it's one of *those* days.
It is *very much* one of those days.
I'm supposed to be in the throne room for the latest reports from the North.

But you're not going.

I could not be *less* interested in the latest reports from the North.
I don't think my body is *capable* of wanting anything less than sitting on that terrible little *throne* that makes my butt go *numb.*
Just to listen to my Dad *yell* at me for not wanting to burn the *Faeriewoods* to the ground.

He's always *horrible* when he's sick, and these days he's *sick* all of the time.
He just wants you to be ready to run the kingdom.

No, he wants me *afraid.* Afraid of every horrible thing that might happen if the *Blood Laws* aren't upheld.
And he's just terrified my *uncle's* going to come out of *hiding* in Northport when he hears he's sick. That he'll make a *claim* for the throne.

Northport's hundreds and hundreds of miles away, and anyway... You're *before* the Duke in the line of *succession.*
Don't *remind* me.

You seem more nervous than normal.
I am.

What is it?

I need to know if I can *trust* you.

What? Of course you can.
Thorn...

Not just in a *regular* way... I know this isn't like...a *normal* friendship. I don't get to have *normal.*
But I *trust* you and I *like* you, and I don't like or trust anybody *else.*

Yorie, I've never heard you talk like this.

I'm sorry... I'm not so good... at emotions.

The Bandaged Man. He's here because he heard about a *plot* in the North. A plot to get me out of Pipetown and off *Esseriel.* So when my father dies, the crown passes to the *Duke.*
That's what he's telling him in the throne room, *right now.*

How...how do you know that?

There's something I need to *talk* to you about.

And then I'm going to ask you the biggest *favor* anybody's ever asked you in your *life.*

→KOF KOFF←
Boy, you should have been at the meeting yesterday. We were speaking of your well-being and your future.
I know. I'm sorry.
What? Get *closer,* boy. I can barely see you.

I'm right here, Dad.
There's that sneering face I know all too well.
I'm not sneering.

You're so small, Yorik. You should go running with the gardener's boy. He's got some *meat* on his bones.
I feel like I could snap you in half with my hand, and I'm a *dying man.*

HAHAHAH--

→KOFFF KOFF KOF KOFF←

Can we get this over with?
I'm dying, boy. I'm *dying* and you can't wait to be *rid* of me.

No, Dad. It's just...
It's **hard.** Doing this every day is hard.

I'm leaving you the ***Last Empire of Man*** in this world. It ***should*** be hard. It will always be hard. But you will rise to meet the challenge.

But you will need to be ***vigilant.*** You will need to ***protect*** them. You know what lurks in those damned forests, outside our walls.
My last wish to you will become ***law,*** and you will uphold it until the last of your days. This is the way of our people.

Tell me you understand this.
I understand, Father.

You will keep the ***Blood Laws.*** You will keep those tainted with the magic wild of the world from mingling with and ***tainting*** the blood of our people.
In doing so, you will keep the old ways, and the old cultures alive. You do it in memory of our ancestors chased out of their homes by twisted weirdblooded monsters.
You will do it in memory of me.

Say you understand and accept.
Yes, Father. I understand and accept.

Basil. I want ***double*** the guards on his room tonight.
If we're lucky I'll pass tonight and we'll be done with this damned ***ritual,*** and I'll be free of this pain in me.
Otherwise, have the boy brought back to me in the morning, and I'll give my ***last wishes*** again.

Yes, Your Majesty. I will see to it.

Get the boy out of my sight, and bring me the Bandaged Man.

The King will see you now.
Thank you, Basil.

Your Highness.

Tomorrow night?
Yes. What did the Cherrywood boy say?

He said... he's thinking about it.

I SMELL TERRIBLE!
That smell's a point of *pride.*
That's the smell of an apprentice in the *Pipetown Engineer Corps.* It cakes on to you and you'll never be fully rid of it.
Breathe it in, Lass.

It's *still* pretty terrible.

Yes, dear, and we'd prefer everyone not vomit over their suppers now, wouldn't we? Go clean up and get ready for the dinner rush.

Oakley.
Tell Wynd not to run off tonight. I need to have a *word* with the both of you.

Okay?

You know the nights I tell you something and you *ignore* it and go off getting into trouble? This is *not* one of those nights.

I mean it, girl. The streets aren't *safe* for him right now.

Yeah, Mom. I've got it.

Wynd?

You smell *terrible.*
So do you!

I smell *regular person* terrible. You smell like somebody used you to clean a *toilet.*
I'm very proud of that smell. All the old fogeys upstairs told me so.

Mom says *family meeting* after the rush.
No spying on *gardeners.*

OAKLEY!

What? I know you. I know where you go.
You could *pretend.*
That wouldn't irritate you nearly enough.

DING!
DING!
Wynd. Orders building up.
Yeah, yeah...

I'm going to take a ***shower*** and try and smell better.
Have ***you*** heard of showers?
Oakley.

I'm leaving!

Actually, hey, can you grab something for me from the ***store room?*** Another slab of butter?
'Course.

FWOOSH!

And they're sure?

Yes, Molly. They're saying he won't last a few more days. Maybe a week.
If it's going to *happen,* it needs to happen *now.*
I understand. There's...something else. A *favor* I'd like to ask--

We're not alone.

I'm sorry.

Wynd? You shouldn't *eavesdrop.*

I wasn't... Titus needs butter.
Darling. It's *fine.* Why don't you come over here...

I do so wish you didn't have to hide them.

Miss Molly?

Keep those *ears* covered and get back up to work now, dear. I'll be up in a moment.

I'm going to have to get a *message* out. But I can't imagine transporting *three* would be any more difficult than two...

Good. When should I expect?
Tomorrow night.
BUTTER
ROYALLY GOOD!

That soon.
Alright, then.

BUTTER

I'll see you bright and early, Miss Molly.
Thank you, dear.
WC

Really. Are you alright? All day you've--
I'm fine, love. Fine. Never you mind.

Okay, go get Wynd.
I'm here!

Yeah, Mom. He's right in ***front*** of you. Have you gone blind?

Oh, yes. There you are.

What are you doing?
Pouring myself a ***tall glass,*** dear. I'll be needing it.

Can I have a tall glass?
Hush.

We need to have a ***hard conversation*** right now.
One I've been ***dreading*** for a very long time.

Tomorrow, I'm making a supply run down to **Southport** through the central transport pipeline. A night run.
A night run? Why--
Just let me get through this, Oakley.

Wynd, I'm going to need you to pack a ***bag.*** Bring only what you ***need.*** What you can carry easily and won't take up much space.

You're going to be coming with me.

What, is he going to use his ***renowned*** haggling skills to get you a good price on ***pork loin?***

No, dear. I'm putting him on a boat to ***Northport.***

NO!

Oakley, please. Don't make this *harder* than it has to be.

Why am I going to Northport?

I have *friends.* They'll set you up with a place to live. They'll treat you well.
I...I won't be coming back?

Oh, no, dear. I'm so sorry, that won't be possible.

But you'll be able to live *openly* there. You won't have to *hide.* Cut your hair. Show those beautiful *ears* of yours.

I don't *want* to show people my ears!

I'm sorry, it's not *safe* for you here anymore. Much as I wish that wasn't the case. Much as I've *prayed* things might change.

It's going to get so much *worse.* Worse in a way I don't think either of you can *understand.*

e King calling the *Bandaged an* down from the North. That's how it began *last time.*
He can *smell* the magic in a person's blood, Wynd. And he loves what he does...It's a *vendetta* of sorts.

They say his family was *killed* in one of the northern magic wars.
He didn't know whether it was the *Faeries* or the *Vampyres* who did it, so his hate turned to all *magic-blooded* people.
He became very good at *killing* them. Good enough to get the attention of the King.

"Before either of you were born, the Duke had been helping magic-blooded people settle in the shadows of Pipetown.
"He found them jobs and homes... Half-Faeries, Quarter-Vampyres, and anyone who had just been touched and changed by the wild magic of the world.
MENU
"The Bandaged Man found them all. Found every person who had helped them hide in the city as well...
"The Duke escaped to Northport, despite the King calling for his head...
"But the others..."

"I still remember the *bodies* piled on the sides of the road."

"And when I found you, months later, on patrol 'round the northern floodgates...
"This beautiful child with *pointed ears...*
"It was *suicide* to take you in, but I couldn't let myself leave you to die.
"I'd sat back and watched too much *death* already."

It's not *fair.*

The world rarely is.

I want to stay *here.* This is my *home.* This is where I *fit in.*

Dear, there's so much of yourself you *don't know.* That you don't understand. I've been *selfish* keeping you this close this long...

Up in the magic north of *Esseriel,* you'll be able to become who you were always *meant* to be.

NO!

Wynd...

Mom.

You know I'm right, dear. He doesn't hear how the people still talk about the weirdbloods. You can't pretend you haven't heard the other engineers say horrible things.
You're too smart to be blind to all that.

It's not that. I want to know why we're just sitting on our asses in a kingdom where they'd just as soon kill someone we love! And when things get bad, we just kick him out and keep going.

There are responsibilities here, dear. You'll understand someday.

I hope I *never* do. I hope I'm never that *selfish.*

You think I wouldn't rather *run off* on a lark?!
You think I don't *dream* of Northport?!

THEN SEND ME WITH HIM!

This isn't a discussion.

No, it sure as hell isn't.

CHAPTER THREE
NORMAL

snf

Hey.

Scoot over. I'm coming in.

Okay. I'm going to say something I don't want to say. I don't even a *little bit* want to say it.

Then don't.

Wynd. She's *right.*
We *both* know she's right.

Oakley...

No, Wynd. Listen...It's *dangerous--*

YOU DON'T THINK I KNOW IT'S DANGEROUS?!

Wynd...

I can ***hear*** them through the spouts, Oakley. I hear them talking ***every single day,*** and I know what they think about people like me.
I know what they'd ***do*** to me if they had the ***chance.***

They're ***wrong...***
They're just ***afraid*** because they don't under-stand they don't need to be...

You don't ***know*** that! You don't know that you shouldn't be afraid...
My ears keep ***growing,*** and who knows what will happen to me next.

It'll keep *infecting* and *twisting* me from the inside out until I'm *something horrible.*
Something even *you* couldn't look at without being *afraid.*

You don't know that...

Magic *spreads,* Oakley! If I go out of Pipetown, where it's *wild* in the world, it's going to spread into *me.*
This...This *thing* in me. That makes my ears look like some kind of *freak* so I can't live a *normal life.*

That's what's wrong with me, Oakley.

It's a part of you...

I DON'T WANT IT TO BE A PART OF ME!
I WANT TO BE NORMAL!

All I want is to wake up one morning and have *small, normal ears,* and regular dreams.

Maybe I could even...*introduce* myself to someone like that boy at the castle. That *gardener.* I don't know his name.
Maybe...Maybe I could *ask* him his name. Maybe we could have a life together.

Wynd...

I know it's impossible. I know I don't get that kind of happy ending...
But I want to *stay* in Pipetown and live a *normal* life.

Promise me you won't make me go.

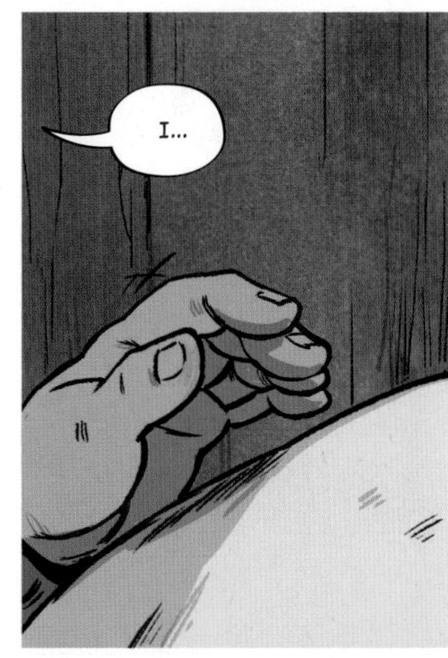
I...

I promise.

CRASH

Huh?

D-Dad? What's going on...

Go back to ***sleep,*** boy. This doesn't ***concern*** you.

No, Thorn.
You should stay
awake.
Please.
Take a seat.

Dad,
are you
o--

That was
not a request.

Ungh

DON'T
YOU TOUCH
HIM!

Then stop playing these little *games* with me, Ash.
I can *smell* it on you. The *stink* of magic.
If you lie to me again, I'm going to have to bring your son in for interrogation.
NO!

If you tell me the *truth* now, all of that can be *averted.* Wouldn't that be marvelous?

A Sprytle...
A Sprytle formed in the green-house...A plant had been neglected. It had gone wild.

And *who* would you say neglected it, Ash?

I did.

The King should have listened to me and **burned** these gardens a decade ago.
I think I'll **remind** him of the suggestion.

With me. We have more to root out tonight.

SLAM!

Dad, are you--
I'm *fine,* boy. I'm fine.

I...I've served the King *loyally* since I was your age. He knows that.

He...He *must* know that.

It's going to be *okay,* Dad.
Everything is going to be okay.

SCRUB
SCRUB

Eya, Wynd. You *listening* over there?
Sorry?

Just need a hand for a second. A couple of them, actually. We've got a *leak* coming on.

Oh...Oh, yeah. Sure.
Never been good with a *wrench,* but if I wait until Oakley gets back from her shift, I'll *never* hear the end of it.

Mr. Titus...

Oh, *"mister,"* am I? Thank you ***very*** much.
Have you... Have you ever met a ***weirdblood?***

What's this now?

I know you've been out of Pipetown. I might...I might have to go soon.
I just wanted to...

Yeah, yeah o'course. I was ***curious*** too when I was a boy.
Thinking about all them ***strange monsters*** up north. The way it gets in you, ***twists*** you up.

Most folks you meet, though, are just people.
They're nice as anyone else, just have a touch of the *strange* to them. A bit of the world *stuck on* where it shouldn't be.

'Course, there are *bad ones,* too.

Was doing a trade run down the *Old Road* from Northport, through the Faeriewoods, and there was this real *scoundrel* on the cart with us.
He'd sneak off the path at night to try and get some bits of *moss* to sell at the black market here in Pipetown, knowing it could get us all *killed.*

One morning he woke up and his right leg was *fully covered* in bark--more than bark, the whole leg was becoming a kind of *living wood.*
He had to convince us to chop the leg off to let him get back in the city, and we did it for him...
And sure as eggs, the next morning he had *flowers* sprouting from his ears.
He'd gone right back out while we were *sleeping,* the leg not even healed, and stumbled into a fresh patch of weird.
Left him at the side of the road, come to think of it, otherwise I doubt we'd've been let back in the city.
Weren't going to get us all *banished* on some weirdblood's behalf.
Why are you asking, boy?

No reason.
The weird's not going to get you in Pipetown, if you're worried.
No. It's not that.
Are you set? I might step out.

Right, right. Sorry for droning on.
It's fine.

Going up looking for your ***girlfriend,*** then? I've seen you blushing.

I, *uh...* I'm just gonna go. Okay?

Ah, to be young.

sigh
PROPERTY OF WYND

WYND!

Oakley? You're supposed to be at--

I know. But I ***heard*** something. Something that could help.

Help what?
I promised you I would find a way. I know we don't have much time...
But I think... I think I might have an answer.

Answer?
The answer. A way to keep my promise...

I don't--
You don't need to understand right now, but you will.

I'm going to tell my mom I'm taking a ***double shift,*** but that's a lie. I need you to follow the pipeline to ***Mid-City*** during the shift changeover.
Tell her you want the night off to pack. Can you do that?

I'll find you at the Key Junction under Oldtown. Under the ***Great Temple.*** Can you get there on your own, or do you need a map?
LIVE

I...I think I can find it.
Okay. ***Good.*** I'll see you then.

LIBRARY
TOWN HALL
KRAB CAFÉ
GONNA BE CLOSED
FOR A FEW DAYS

THE DARK SPOUT
FOOD ALL DAY
-
BEER ON TAP
GONNA BE CLOSED
FOR A FEW DAYS

What's *this* now, Molly?
Sorry, Henry. You know I *close* when I need to do a *restock* down from Southport.

Oh, what'd a few *beers* cost ya? I don't like the other taverns. They all give me the evil eye.

Maybe you've earned it, Henry.
I *have* earned it. But you still treat me sweetly.

Clearly I've treated you *too* sweetly. Go to the Drip Room. Tell Gordon to buy you a pint on me.
Will he listen?

Can't hurt to try.
HAPPY HOU

Wynd, boy... I just shut the doors for the night...
How's your packing going?

Wynd?
LIVE

WYND?!

Should have just clunked him on the head and dragged him off in the night. That's what I get for telling him nicely...

Titus.
Almost done in here, Miss Molly. We'll have the Spout up in a jiff--
Wynd is **gone.** Oakley too, no doubt.
I need you to **bring them back** home. I need you to do it **quick.**

Oh, they're just a couple of ***teenagers*** being fools. They'll come back around--

Titus, I need you to listen to the ***tone*** in my voice right now.
Yes, ma'am.

Bring my children home.

Yes, ma'am.

We're going to need to move quickly.

I'll need to be ***back*** in the castle before they realize anything is ***wrong.***
Do you have ***every-thing*** you need?

It's a big ask, rince Yorik. You're sking that boy to ***give his life up*** or you. And this ourney won't be an easy one.
I still... I ***thought*** he'd come. I didn't think...
I didn't think I'd have to do this ***alone.***

You don't.

You're late, boy. We were about to *leave* without you.
I doubt it. That'd mean Yorie would have to carry his own bags.
Thorn.
If you ever leave me *waiting* like that again, I'm going to have you *hanged.*
I think you're plenty on your way to getting me hanged already.
It's *now or never.* Are you ready, boys?
Ready as I'll ever be.
Let's go.

BOLTS

3

NORTH RIVER

There you are.

I don't *understand...* Why are we out here?
Isn't this... Isn't this dangerous?
Yeah. That's *why* you need to *follow* me.

Wait, is anybody watching?

No. I don't *think* so?

Okay, here. Get in *quick,* before anyone sees us.

SLAM!

Wh-what? What is this place...?
Am I stepping in *poop?*
Oakley, I *swear,* if I'm stepping in poop...

KLIK
Oh, sorry. I'm kinda *used* to the dark.
There. Is that better?

I mean, *maybe?* What's going on, Oakley?
I overheard one of the other workers whispering at lunch. About the catacombs under the *Old Temple to the Four Winds.*

They said that that's where the *weirdbloods* were hiding.
Weirdbloods... Why would I want...?

He said the rumor was there was *some-body* down in the tunnels.
Somebody who could take the weird *out* of their blood.
Some kind of *witch.*

That sounds like a *bedtime* story.
Yeah, I thought so, too...
But then I went to the *pipe system* right above where we are now...

And I could hear *whispers.*

Do...Do you see that?

N
W
E
S

It's the story of *Esseriel.* Do you know it?

Sorry! We know we shouldn't be--
No, no... I didn't mean to scare.
But the story...Do you know it?

I...They told us in school... But...
You are on the right path. I'll walk with you a ways, if you don't mind...
I can make sure you get to her. Get to the witch.

Thank you so much--
Please... I do not care for the light. Just keep walking ahead of me.

There were once four great races of human-kind, and by the grace of the Winds, our species ruled over this world.

"The North Men ruled over the frosty forests of the Borean Waste, by the grace of the ***North Wind*** and all its cold, powerful tempests.
"The West Men ruled over the Sunset Peaks, by the grace of the ***West Wind*** and its warm, calming breezes.

"The East Men ruled over the Skydrenched Isles, by the grace of the *East Wind* and its cooling, life-bringing rains.
"And the South Men ruled over the scorching deserts of the Notunlands, by the grace of the *South Wind* and its sandstorms..."

"Once a generation, the Winds would call their children together from the four corners of the world, to meet on the island they called their home.
"Esseriel.
"They were proud of what their respective empires had built, and so they shared the fruits of their kingdoms, and their latest discoveries of the world...
"These meetings brought a great peace, and a dream of a united world, where all races of man would come together on Esseriel and rule it.
"They say the Winds promised to give their children the gift of flight, and mastery over the air, should they come home to them."

"But the Empires of Man had more to explore, more to discover, and so, time after time, they set off back to their corners of the world.
"And so the Winds let their children go forth into a world, not knowing the danger that awaited them.
"Because there was another force in this world. A darker, stranger force...
"A god of the wild wood, who envied the freedom of man to go from place to place...
"And envied the Winds most of all. For their power, and for the devotion man had bestowed upon them."

"And so the God of the Wild Wood unleashed his *wrath* upon the world.
"He corrupted all growing things so that they would *spawn* its monstrous children.
"The terrible *Sprytles,* who with a single touch could twist a man's blood into something strange... Something *weird.* Marking them of the earth and not of the air.
"And so new races were born...
"The *Faerie* of the deep forest, with their monstrous claws and terrible wings...
"And the *Vampyre* of the rock-strewn deserts, with their pale skin and razor teeth.
"The human kingdoms began to *fall,* one by one, across the world.
"In time, the Men of the East and the West *stopped coming* to the meetings on Esseriel."

"The Four Winds implored the Empires of the North and South to *retreat* to their embrace. To *fortify* with their power. To become their *children* as they had long promised.
"But the men were proud. They had built great wealth and power and wanted to *keep* it. They decided to fight.
"But the God of the Wild Wood was too strong...
"And in time, the last cities fell..."

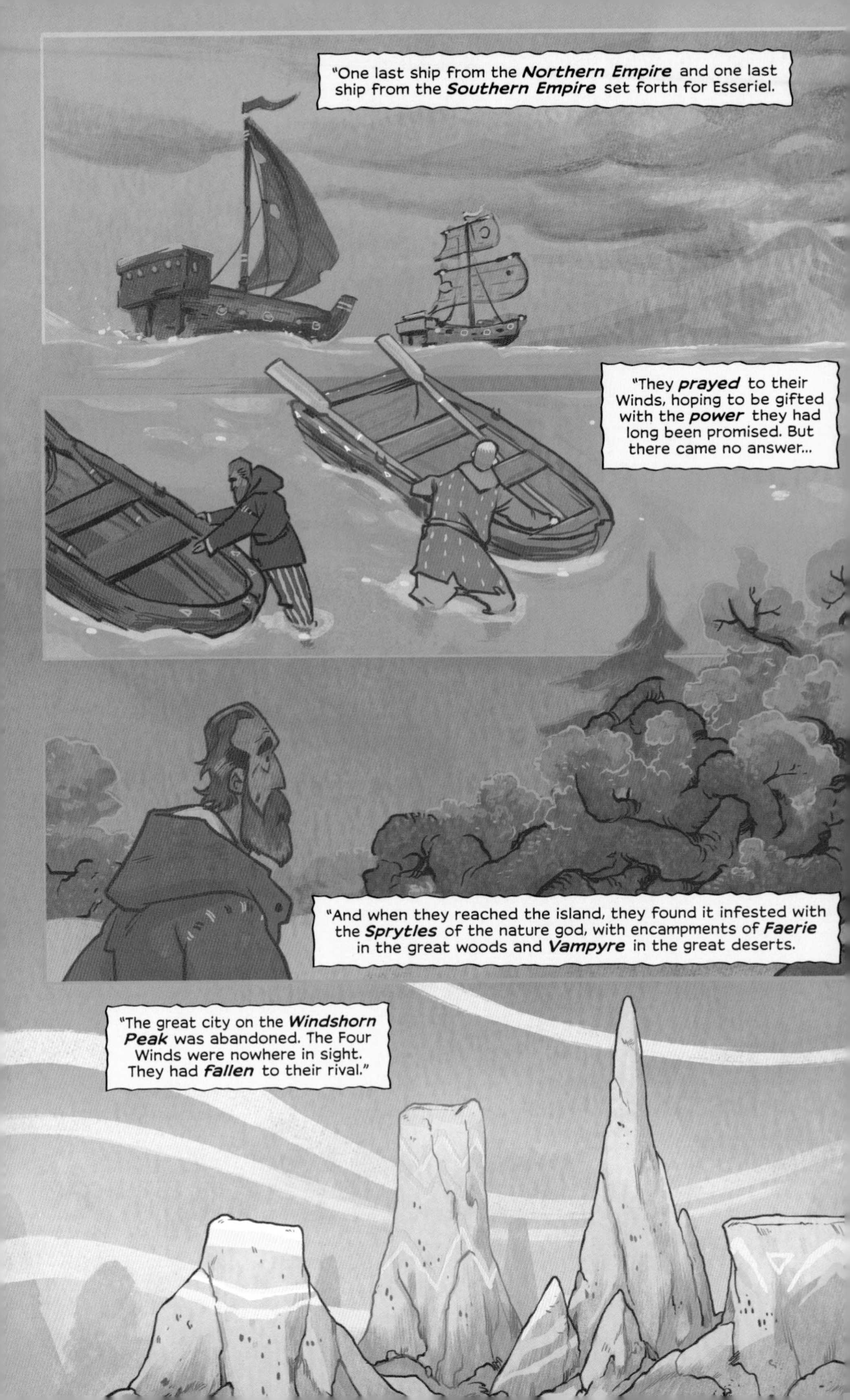
"One last ship from the Northern Empire and one last ship from the Southern Empire set forth for Esseriel.
"They prayed to their Winds, hoping to be gifted with the power they had long been promised. But there came no answer...
"And when they reached the island, they found it infested with the Sprytles of the nature god, with encampments of Faerie in the great woods and Vampyre in the great deserts.
"The great city on the Windshorn Peak was abandoned. The Four Winds were nowhere in sight. They had fallen to their rival."

"The remnants of the two empires built a great walled city to ***protect*** them from the corrupting wild nature of the world.
"What we now call ***Pipetown,*** but is known formally as the ***Last Empire of Man.***
"The children of the two dynasties wed and created the ***bloodline*** that sits on the throne to this day, with the great ***King Yossar*** and his son, ***Yorik.***
N
S
"And those of magic blood were ***banned*** from the city to protect the last ***true humans*** in this world."

Is that... Is that all real?
So they say. That is why the King holds the **Blood Laws** so dearly. That is why I have come here tonight.

Do you have... Are your **ears** pointy, too?

Yes, child... My ears are pointed...

Quite a bit *more* than that, too.

Anyways...

CHAPTER FOUR
DESCENT

We're here.

COUGH!

W-what...What happened to him?
Didn't *survive* the process...Too much blood lost...

Wynd... Maybe this was a *bad idea...*Maybe we should go back...
No. If they're all here, there has to be some *truth* to it, right?

We can't go back. Not when we're so close.

Next...

I, *uh*...
I want to see her. The witch.
Affliction? You don't seem like much...

It's a...
It's my ears. But that's just the ***start,*** right?

Trying to catch it early. Yes. It's wise...
You have the ***fee?***

Fee? I don't have any...

Yeah. I have it.

Oakley, that's like ***four months'*** pay...
Five, actually.

A promise is a promise, right?

I don't want to ***lose*** you. Okay?

Okay.

This way.

I'm coming with him.

As you wish...

Oh god, I think I'm going to throw up...
What's ***happening*** to them?!

It's called ***transfusion.***
It's a technique I developed in North-port...

HOW TO
We draw out the ***weirdblood*** and supplant it with ***healthy,*** human blood. It can take some time...

But perhaps a little *less* with you.
This is all of him? No *fur?* No *flowers?* No *branches?*
No branches.

You're the *witch?*

I'm a *doctor.* My name is *Myr.* I came down to Pipetown a year ago to try and help the weirdblood population...

Do you know what did this to you? What kind of *Sprytle?*
There are different kinds?
Sure. Yeah. *Loads* of them.

I dunno. I've had the ears since I was a *baby,* but they're getting *longer* as I get older.
And there's no other symptoms?
I...I have bad dreams.
Ts! Ts!

I have bad dreams, too.

Here, I can *test* you.
I've been *classifying* the different *breeds...*Hold out your finger.
KEEP OUT!
My *finger?*

...CH!

Gotcha.

Now let's see what kind of *weirdblood* you've got.

This is all so *gross* I can't even handle it.
I can deal with gross if it means I can stay here. In Pipetown. Live *openly,* with you and Miss Molly.

This is every-thing I ever *dreamed* of.
Thank you, Oakley. Thank you *so much* for finding this place. I don't know what I would do without you.

By the winds... This isn't *possible.*

AIIEEEE!!!

When the King alerted me that the Prince had been *kidnapped* from the castle, I suspected we'd find some secret *encampment.*
I promised him I would *find* it. And I am a man of my *word.*
I knew there was a *stink* coming up through the *cracks...*

ou should have tried to ave. I likely would have ught you, but a few of ou might have gotten over the walls.
Some of you may have even been able to *dodge* my riflemen. But thankfully you rounded yourselves up, nice and easy.

Orders, sir?

Kill them. All the weirdbloods and their foul handlers. We cannot risk *contamination* spreading.

Wynd, take my hand...

But Myr...
No buts. We have to ***GO!***

She's right. You need to go, ***now.***
And we need to get as ***many*** people out of here as we can...

We need to ***collapse*** the tunnels. ***Lock*** them away from us.
Yes, Myr. At once.

You need to survive. I need you to *promise* me you'll survive.
W-why...

You're not like the rest of them. Find my *sister* in Northport. She'll explain. You need to get out of this city.
NOW.

Is there a way into the main pipe system?
Three lefts and a right.
May the winds bless your journey, young man. It's going to be a *long one,* I'm afraid...But it could change *everything.*

THEY HAVE A BATTERING RAM!
RUN, CHILDREN! YOU HAVE TO RUN!

We can't just let them die!

I can't save them, but I can save ***you,*** if we leave ***now.***
I can take us through the secondary line, back to the Dark Spout. It's going to be grimy but I can get us there.

...Okay.

Okay, let's go.

What's *this* now...?
SNIF
This blood is *fascinating...*
I'll have to introduce myself to it *personally.*

Why is this *happening...?*
I think he said the *Prince* was kidnapped.

But *why* is this happening?
I don't know, Wynd. I really don't.

Okay. We need to get above ground, now.
We'll stay in the *shadows.* We can move with the *crowds.* You need to keep your hood up, okay?

Okay.
Just don't say anything, and follow me. I'm going to get you home.

You two.
Stop.

We're just wrapping our shift. Just want to get home.
He doesn't look like he's in the Corps.

He got his worksuit drenched so bad the shift leader decided to burn it.
Don't get too close or you'll get a whiff.

I want you to take the hood off, boy.

Trust me, you don't want--

SHUT UP!
THOK

DON'T HURT HER!

It's okay, I can...take off the hood...
Just let her go.
Don't, Wynd. Don't.

You don't want her. You want me.

Fair enough.

And what's the *meaning* of this, now? Terrorizing *children?*
Yer bad enough as it is, without *bothering* innocent--

Oh.

Stand back and let me do my job.
5

Nah, don't think I will.

SMASH

I'm sorry.
I'm sorry too, for that matter.

Get yerself to the ***Spout.*** And hurry. I'll make enough of a ***mess*** to turn them around a beat.

They'll ***kill*** you.

Yer mam told me to get her children home, and no ***bootlickers*** are going to stand in the way of my doing just that.

Now ***run,*** girl.

NO WEIRD BLOOD
ACORN AVENUE

SLAM!

I feel... like my ***chest*** is going to explode.

It's okay.

WHAT ABOUT THIS IS OKAY?!

You're still *alive!* That's okay!

We can *still* get you out.

Where's Mom?

Mom!
Miss Molly?

Mom, are you...?!

Hush, dear.

What are *they* doing here? Who are they?!
This is my *house!* Who are *you?!*

I don't even know how to answer that question.
Thorn, *kill them.* We can't allow witnesses.
I'm not going to kill them.
Well, do *something?*

Stop, Yorik. Look at how *scared* they are.
Well, I'm scared too.

You're the gardener.

Really. You know who *he* is?
Why do you know who I am?

I don't know!

Are you okay? Are you in one piece...?
Titus...He helped make a *distraction.*
Bless him. I hope he's all right.

I don't think...

Let's not go there, love. We need to make *quick strides* if we're going to make it to Southport by *sunrise.* I've packed the boat already.
The Duke's Men will take them out to sea. Our *contact* should be waiting at the mouth of the tunnel.

You've been with the *Duke's Men* all this time.

Not as long as I *should* have been.
We'll have a nice long chat about it when I'm back, and then you can *apologize* to me for being so cruel.

Wynd, I packed a few things for you. I'm *sorry.* There's no time to swap them out. We need to leave now.

Oakley, you'll have to make your *goodbye* quick...

I'm sorry. I'm sorry I made you promise...
I'm sorry...

I...I...

RRRRiiNG!!!
Who is it...?
It's probably nothing. Just a ***bar fly*** ignoring the closed sign.

BANG! BANG!
THUNK!
That doesn't ***sound*** like a fly.

Stay hidden.

Hello? Is someone there...?

Yes. *Someone* is.

I'm...I'm afraid we're *losed* for the evening.

Oh, I'm sure we could make an *exception,* couldn't we?
We've been at it *all night,* and I'm rather parched.

An exception, then. I'm afraid the *kitchen* is closed, but I suppose I can pour a few *flagons* for the King's Men.
Do *all* the men get some, or just the Captain?

Oh, let's make it a party.
We could even invite whoever's *spying* on us from the doorway.

Sorry... I heard voices.

It's okay, dear. These kind men just needed a ***drink.*** There's nothing to worry about.
I...I can help.

No...Oakley, my sweet. I'm going to need you to do me a ***big favor,*** while I help these men.

I think I'm not going to be able to run that ***errand*** I was talking about after all.
Why don't you ***take care*** of it for me?

Mom.

That wouldn't be a *problem* now, would it?
She just needs to run down and get the *package* from the pantry. Then she'll be on her way.

Oh, certainly. We wouldn't want to *inconvenience* you.

I'm not sure I know the way.
Oh, I'm sure you'll *manage.* You're a bright girl.

That's why I *love* you so much.

I'll...I'll be right back up, then.

SNiF

What's wrong?

Yorik.
It's *crying.*

It's bad, huh?
Follow me.

What? No. We're not going *anywhere.* Your mom--
Is pouring beer for the *Bandaged Man.*
She's...not coming.

No.

We have to be fast.

Why did I do this... Why did I...?
There isn't time for that now. We need to keep going.

Girl, what's *your name?*
Oakley.

Thank you, Oakley. I promise he's not as *horrible* as he seems.
He better be *worth* all this.

I can only promise not as horrible.
I'm *Thorn Cherrywood.* How about you?
I'm...I'm *Wynd.*

Then you stay at our backs. We need some *wind power* right now. Okay?

Okay.

See. This is my *favorite* part.

I'm sorry?

It's the *chase.* It's no fun when they know they can't get away. No *thrill* to the hunt.
You need to offer a little *hope,* that they might see tomorrow.
Otherwise there's no *art* to it. It's just *blood.*

I...I don't know what you're talking about.

Oh, I think you *do.*
THUMP!

Not that it matters, anymore. Not to you.
SHNK.
gguck

SPOUT
GONNA BE CLOSED
FOR A FEW DAYS

VRR!
Okay.
THE DARK SPOUT
DOWN TOWN
These tunnels *echo.* So the key is being absolutely quiet.
We don't want to make any sound that will draw anyone's attention.
If we can do that, we ***might*** just make it out of this tunnel alive.

SOUTH
PORT

I'm not sure I know the way.
Oh, I'm sure you'll ***manage.*** You're a bright girl.
That's why I ***love*** you so much.

SOUTH PORT
VRRRRR

Can this thing go any *faster?*
Not without getting a lot more attention than we want.
We're a trade ship, we're going to market for...I don't know. Pork loin or something. We need to look as *bored* and *tired* as everyone else.

I hate this.
Thorn, I hate this.
I know, buddy.

Are you okay?

No.
Do you think your mom...?
I can't think like that--
I'm sorry. I shouldn't have made you promise to help me...This is my fault.

I can't comfort you right now, Wynd. I'm doing everything in my power not to strangle His Highness over there, and not scream and cry.
I don't blame you for what's happening, but I can't hold your hand through it.
O-okay.

WHUMP
SOUTH PORT
Oof!

Oh, gross.
Yorie...
No, look at his ears! They're pointy.

He's a weirdblood.

I'm sorry. He doesn't know how to be a *real person* yet.
What?!

Quiet.

Stop *telling* me to be quiet. Stop *bossing* me around.
Are you even older than me? You're just a *kid.* You don't know any-thing.

I'm not being crazy. The Bandaged Man can *smell* weirdbloods. How do you think he *found* us at that fat lady's bar?

Shut him up. *Now.* Or I will.

No! Listen to me. I am trying to do a *good* thing here. I am trying to make the Blood Laws go away so your friend doesn't get *murdered!*
But that won't happen, if he gets us *all* murdered!

He's right.

No. He's *not* right.

I don't want anyone else to get hurt because of me. I can lead them off the trail...

Thorn, I want you to hit them *both* very hard on the head so they *shut up* and stop being stupid.

I think we missed our chance at not being found.

RRRRRR!!!

There...the *motorboat...* Get me close enough to get onboard.
Yes, sir!
VRR

Okay. *Move.*
What are you doing?
You wanted to see if this boat could go faster?

I'm making it go *faster.*

VRRROOM!

If the Bandaged Man is already here, then the *King's Men* will be waiting for us in Southport! We're *surrounded!*
The *contact* we were supposed to meet at the end of the pipeline is probably already *captured.*

This has all gone to *pieces.* I'm going to be taken back, my dad's going to die, and he'll make me keep the *Blood Laws* alive another generation.
Everyone will *hate* me and there's no way out...

What about those?

Those are for overspill. They dump out into the undergrowth.
Out of the pipes?
Yeah. Out of the pipes.

What?

No. No, *absolutely* not.
This is all my *stuff!*

Okay. We need to jump and swim to the edge. Keep our heads just *under* the water until they pass. They'll keep following the boat.
Hands around my *shoulders,* Yorik. Hold on tight.

I'm going to take hold of *you,* too. I know you can't swim.
Hey! I can *kind of* swim.

Then I'll only kind of hold you. We jump on three...
One...
Two...

JUMP

SPLASH

SOUTH PORT
VRRRRRRRRR

A-3

I liked **all** of that stuff.
It's just **stuff,** Yorik. You can get **more** stuff.

Wow...

It's a *jungle...*

No, I think it's a ***marshland.***
This type of fern... We have it up in the ***greenhouse.*** Not wild like this of course, but my Pop used to say they grew up and down the ***rivers*** of Esseriel.

And this...This would have been its ***Great River,*** way back when, before they ***contained*** it. To keep out the wild.
Don't let the ***plants*** touch you, best as you can.

You can get down now.
Absolutely not.

Where do we go...?
I guess... we keep walking south.

Wait! Stop.

GEEEBO!

What is it...?
It's a **Sprytle...** You don't want to let it touch you, or it could taint you with its magic.
I thought they were supposed to be **monsters...**

Yeah. That's what I thought, too.
But they're kind of **cute,** right?

Cute or not, I've **seen** what they do to people. Let's keep **moving.**

I agree with Pointy Ears. I don't like this one bit.

Stand back! I won't let you turn me into a tree monster!

Why are they *following* me?!

They can taste the *magic* in you. They know you're one of them.
Please stop being *terrible.*
I refuse!

Wait. *Stop.*
Do you hear that?
Yeah.

I don't hear anything.
Yeah, nothing but the *sound* of your own voice.
Hey!

Yorik. Quiet...It's getting closer. It's a kind of *buzzing.*

Whoa.

I worried you had slipped out of my grasp, little ones.

The Duke sends his regards.

You...you're the *contact?* The one we were meant to meet in Southport?

I saw the King's Men gathering and suspected something had gone *amiss.* I heard one of them say that the Prince had been *kidnapped.*
I've been following your *caged river* for miles, hoping for some sign.
The Winds have guided m
to you, and I a
grateful.

You...you know my uncle.
Yes, my child. I have known the *Duke* for many, many years. He is a very kind man, and very eager to see you again.

Where is the *woman,* Molly?

She...The Bandaged Man got her.

She's your mother.

Yes.

I *understand,* child.

And my heart *bleeds* for you.

You have had a long enough night as it is. You all look *exhausted,* and worn down.
It would be *hours* to Southport, and we know the guard is already raised. I suggest we *camp* here, and set out at first light.

But...isn't that *dangerous?* The Sprytles?

They are the *children* of these forests. It is a travesty what generations of *neglect* and *refuse* have done to them.
Left them strange and formless... It is no *wonder* you fear them so. But they are kind creatures that wish you no ill...

They do not like the *fir* so as long as I keep it you have *nothing* t worry about.

CHAPTER FIVE
THE WAY OF THE WORLD

You should *sleep,* child.
I tried.

You're the boy the barkeep asked to bring along on the journey.
Yep. That's me.

May I see your *ears?*
Forgive me if it is *rude* to ask in your culture.
No...it's okay.

They are *noble* ears. Magic is rarely so *symmetrical.*
Thank you. I think?

I am sorry the world is this way...That you must *run* like this.
It's not your fault.

Is everyone...
Is everyone like you up there?

No, child. Not in Northport.
I am *Faerie,* Lady Gwendolyn of the Eastwood. A general in the *Great Wars.*

There are wars?
Oh, yes. We've been at war with the *Vampyres* to the west of the Windshorn Peak for a very long time. Since the *Winds* walked the earth.

I didn't think magic folk liked the Winds. I thought the Winds just liked people.

I don't look like *people* to you?

I don't...
You know what I mean. Non-magic people. Humans.
The Winds smile on *all* their children. They are the way of the world. They touch us all.

I heard this story...
I have heard it, too.
I am some twisted *thing* of the North, come to drag you into the woods and make you change into a *monster.* Or so I hear.

Truth is, outside of Pipetown, my people don't think about humans much unless they are in our midst.
Really?

Child, you have much to learn of the world. In the meantime, do not take cruel myths to heart. Stories are *powerful.* They reach inside you and *twist* your way of seeing things.

It sounds like *magic.*
It *is* magic.

Magic is the way the world **touches** you, and changes you into who it needs you to be. Some of those changes are ***frightening,*** but many of them are beautiful.
It is the way of the world. It is not good. It is not evil. It simply is.

You're so frightened.

I don't know who I'll be on the other side. What kind of...person...or thing I'm going to become.

Child. ***None*** of us know.

He was meant to be a gardener.
He was meant to be King.
She, a barmaid.
What will they become in Northport? What shapes will they or their lives take?

It's ***different.***
I know what you mean, but it isn't.

Still. You should get some sleep. Tomorrow will be a long day.

She's cool, huh?
The general?
Yeah.

I heard you two talking last night.
Yeah.

We're doing this *together,* you know?
I talked to her, and I'm going to be coming with you, to *Northport.* She says it's probably too dangerous to go home now.

I'm *glad* you're coming.

Because you're too *scared* to talk to Thorn by yourself.
Well, yeah. Obviously.

Hm. This isn't good.

What's not good?
I did not think they would be able to mobilize so quickly.

PIPETOWN
SOUTH PORT MART

Look closely, boy. Southport is *crawling* with the King's Men.
NO ENTRANCE

PIPETOWN

Is it *over,* then? How can we get to the ship if we can't get to the dock?
The ship isn't at the dock, it's a mile offshore. The plan was to take a smaller boat out... but we can't risk it.

I can fly you out, one by one.
What?!
It will take *time,* but I can do it. You can hide up on the cliffs, overlooking South-port, and I'll take you each in turn.

That sounds *insane.* What if you *drop* us?

I will not drop you.

Yorik should go *first.* If him getting off this island is so important, he should go first.

What if they *see* her and shoot her out of the sky?
I think you're over-thinking this...

No. The Prince is *right.* We must handle this delicately.
Pointy Ears goes last. We don't want to risk the Bandaged Man getting a whiff.

I can go first.
No! Don't leave me with *them.*

Ugh. Fine. I can go first.

Try not to *kill* them, okay? I'm going to want something to do on the boat to Northport.

That rock there. One hour. Maybe less.
We'll be there.

She's going to drop her.
She wouldn't have *offered* if she was worried about dropping any of us.

If she drops her, I hope it's right on the Bandaged Man's head.

KerrrSPLATT!
Right, Thorn?

I think you probably shouldn't talk about his friend like that.
Oh, *come on.* I'm trying to lighten the mood.

I'm doing this to *save* eople like you, emember? So ods forbid, ou let me have a sense of humor...

There were *dozens* of people like me in the tunnels under the Great Temple. Trying to get a *witch* from Northport to clean their blood so they could keep living in Pipetown.
When you *escaped,* the Bandaged Man went there with his soldiers and *killed* all of them. I don't think any-body escaped but Oakley and me.
I *watched* a bunch of them die.

And then it took an ordinary *cook* throwing himself between us and one of those soldiers' *blades* to get us home.

Where the *woman* who took me in as a baby, the mom of the girl you're talking about going kersplat, was probably *killed,* just to get you out of the city.

I'm...

I didn't know.

Then you should keep your mouth *shut* more often and *listen.*

We need to get up to that rock and take *cover.* The longer we're out in the open the more dangerous it all gets.

We've searched every boat that's come through the pipeline for hours...
I think they may have doubled back, into Pipetown.

No. They wouldn't have. There's too much at stake.

SNIF

Sir...
It's that blood...That interesting blood.
Where are...?

They're in the hills overlooking Southport.
Are you sure? It's wild up there.

Don't question me, boy. The Prince is up there, and he's not alone.
GET THE OTHERS.

I think...
I'm going to
throw up.

I would
appreciate if
you didn't.
I'm not
going to
make any
promises.

Can...can
I ask you a
question?
Of course.

Is it really
safer for ***magic-
blooded*** people
up in Northport?

You're
afraid for
your
friend.

I just...
My whole life
people have been
so ***afraid*** of people
like him, and I've
done everything
I can to keep
him ***safe...***
I'd just hate
if we got up there
and it was the same.
If him living in the open
was just some kind of
children's story my
mom would tell us
growing up.

I won't *lie* to you, child. Your kind...You have always succumbed to your basest fears. And it would be a lie to say that there is none of that *fear* in Northport.
But it is *better.* And those touched by magic do live *openly* and well. They might not be welcome on every doorstep...
But few are.

Okay.

You are a very sweet child.
I can feel the *agony* in you. The weight of the loss you are trying your hardest to ignore is more than you can bear, and *still* your mind goes to your friend.

You *love* him.

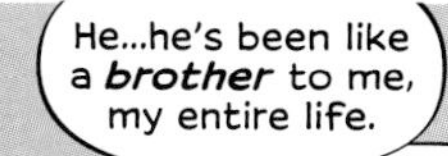
He...he's been like a *brother* to me, my entire life.
He's just... sweet. He's not *hard* like the rest of the world, and I don't want him to change.

You can't stop change, dear. It is the way of the world.
You're afraid you'll lose the version of him you love.
Yeah.

You are *very* sweet. But you are also very ***young,*** and this world will change you and him both in so many incredible ways.
And you'll do that together.

Oh... Oh wow.
I can see Pipetown from up here.

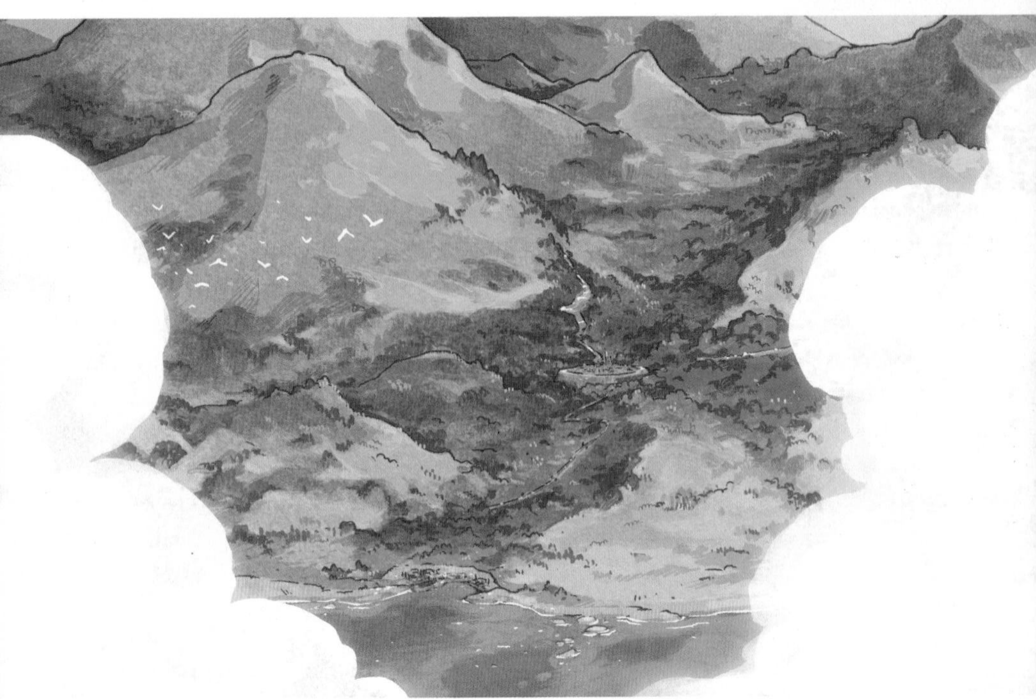

It looks... it looks so small.

Child, it looks that way because it *is* small. The world is so much larger than you know. Larger than even I know.
Now, hold tight. The Duke's ship is just ahead.

Why am I like this?
Honestly, Yorie? I think you need to answer that question yourself.

Hey, Wynd...
Are you okay?

Hah.
Yeah. Dumb question.

Ah, this is all so stupid.
I'm sorry?

You go ***running*** in the late mornings, every day.

How do you know that?

Because every day, I used to go up to this silly little *crow's nest* on top of the Dark Spout with my *tele-scope,* and I would watch you run.

And I would picture that someday, I'd wake up and my ears would be *regular,* and I would get a regular job, doing regular things, and I'd pick up *flowers* from you at the market.
And you'd tell me the things you *knew* about the flowers, and help me pick just the *right* ones.

And maybe you'd ask me to have *dinner* with you or some-thing silly like that.

And that's usually the part of my fantasy where I'd hear the *bell* and need to get back down to the restaurant for the lunch rush.
And my ears would still be pointed, and I'd still be the kid who could never go outside, never go to school, never have a job.

Never meet a nice boy.

Maybe you can have that, in Northport.
Yeah. Maybe.

...Do you know what that is?
What?

That *flower,* right there.
No. I've never seen a real flower up close.

My dad called it a *Winter's Rose.*
He said it was his favorite flower, but it's actually a weed. It's this *tough* little thing that, if it survives long enough, *blossoms* this perfect shade of blue.

That's pretty cool.
Right?

I'm sorry you didn't get that life. And I'm sorry that Yorik is being so mean.
He's been *locked* in a tower for a long time, by himself. And I've been the only one who *talks* to him instead of yells at him.
And he's probably doing this more because he's *afraid,* than because he's brave. But he's still doing it. And it'll still make this world a little bit better.

You're really nice.
Thanks.

Wanna have *dinner?* When we get on the ship?
I know there are other people and stuff there, too, but we could have dinner.

Okay. Let's have dinner on the ship.

Okay.

Something's wrong.

The King's Men.

I'll try and get them to search the next hill. I won't let them see her coming, okay?

No. Don't do this.
I'll come back. But he can smell my *blood.* I can lead him in another direction. I can get him away.
If anything happens, take care of *Oakley.* Make sure she gets to Northport.

Wynd, stop...
You already gave me a little bit of *normal.* It was nice. Even for a few minutes.

Stay out of sight!

I don't see them...I think Wynd's plan ***worked.*** They're heading in another direction.

What do you think is going to happen to him?

You ***care*** all of a sudden?

I...
I ***do*** care. I don't want him to get hurt.

But he's just a *little kid.* He's not going to outrun the Bandaged Man. He's going to *die* out in those woods, trying to give us the time we need to get free.

Yeah. You're probably right.

How many people are going to die because I did this...Because I tried to run?
I don't know.
I didn't think. Not really. Not until he said all that.

Do you really think that nice *fat lady* is dead?

You have to *stop* calling her that. Her name was Miss Molly. Hopefully it *still* is.
Do you think that's why that *mean girl* hates me?
It'd help if you learned their names, buddy. And stopped being horrible.

I know.

Yorik, look...
I know you better than anyone.

When all is said and done, people are going to *love* you and what you did. You giving up the throne to your uncle will make a lot of people's lives *much* better.
They're going to tell stories about how *brave* you are, and how *noble.*

But we both know you're not doing this because you're an *idealist.* You're doing it because you were *afraid.* And that's okay.

But you need to start acting like the *Prince* they're going to write those stories about.
You need to *stop* making the people risking their lives for you *hate* your guts.

SNIF

Do you have something, sir?
No. Keep searching the hills. I have a matter to attend to.
Sir?

I am going to relieve myself and I would like to do it in private.

Oh. Uh...
Sorry, sir. I'll, uh...be going.

That was a little lie.

Why don't you step out of the ***shadows,*** young man? Let me see you.

I'm *not* giving up my friends.
You can *kill* me if you want.
Oh, I *know* that.

I have this *nightmare,* sometimes.
Where I wake up, in the middle of the night, and I'm no longer human.

My face *twists* into this horrible beak and my teeth fall out. And these huge *wings* start ripping out from my back, and it *hurts* worse than anything I've felt in my life.
And then my *friend* comes into my room, and she doesn't recognize me. She thinks I'm some kind of *horrible* thing that killed the person she cares about.
And she starts *beating* me to death with a wrench. And every time she does, I've always been *glad.*
Because if I was going to be some *monster,* twisted up by magic, unrecognizable to the people I love, I would *rather* have been dead.

That's what people like you do. They make people so ***afraid*** of what they're going to become, they would rather ***die*** than become it.

But I want a ***different*** dream.

Child.
You're ***still*** afraid. You'd still rather die. That's the whole ***point*** of this, isn't it?

Yeah. I guess so.

Sit down with me a moment.

I saw you *kill* a lot of people...

I'm sure you did.

You were down there, under the *temple.* You wanted to clean your *blood.* Not be magic.
What if I told you I could take you somewhere, *purify* you, and give you back your life in Pipetown?

Why would you do that? You *hate* people like me.
I don't hate *anybody,* boy. Hate is a *base* emotion.

It's much more *human* than I am.

You're... You're magic.
I was born in the Vampyre caves to the west. I was raised to hunt, and I am rather good at it.
"I thought... magic people killed your family."
"No, King Yossar just wanted me for my natural abilities to help weed out the weird in his midst. He paid me well, and I enjoyed the job.
"The only thing I needed to promise was that none of the humans know what I really was. But why would that matter to me?
"Show up in some bandages to hide your skin from the sun and everyone gets a little creative. But it's never been about hate.
"I do what I do to keep every-one where they belong. Humans behind their walls. Faeries in their forests. Vampyres in their caves.
"As the world should be. Everyone playing their part."

The Faerie said that *magic* is how the world touches and changes you into who you *need* to be.

That's *nonsense.* Who needs to be anything? You're just a little *fry cook.* You're not going to make a difference in this world.
So why not make it easy?

Here, I'll sweeten the pot. You tell me where the Prince is, and where your ship is, and I'll get them *myself.* I won't even tell them about our deal.
The girl will *beg* for your life, and I'll grant her the *kindness,* to show the King's mercy.

You're lying.

If I'm lying then you're already *dead,* and I'm just playing with my food.

I'm not going to help you.

You *already* helped me.
I didn't know about the *Faerie.* Now I know how they're getting to the ship.

No.

It's too late, boy. We have **bowmen** with us. The bug's already dead.

NO!!

Tell the archers to aim for the **sky.** Look for something humanoid on approach.

Come on, Wynd...Come back...Please come back...
I can see her.
-Sigh-
Okay, you go *next,* and then...

Steady.

Fire.

FTNG

FSHH!
THUNK

No...
NO!

The *Weirdblood* is getting away!

Sir?
Oh, he'll be *dessert,* once we've got the future *King* in hand.

Unnnh...

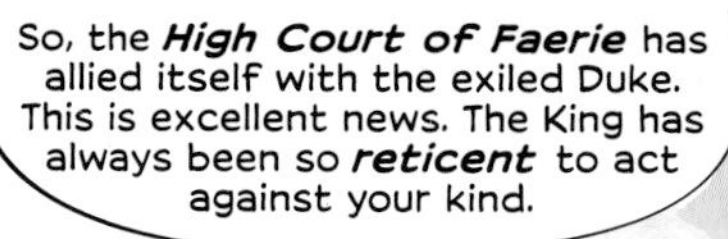

So, the *High Court of Faerie* has allied itself with the exiled Duke. This is excellent news. The King has always been so *reticent* to act against your kind.

I'll make sure to send your *love* when I lead his men to burn the *Faeriewoods* to the ground.

Long live the Duke. Long live Esseriel United!

PTOO!

HA HA

KRK

Get OFF of her!

Ha! This is some kind of joke.

You will stop this at once.

You are a petulant brat. Your father would have given anything to have had a son with a backbone, rather than a sniveling coward.
You realize that, right?

Where is the boy. Wynd?
What have you done with him?

Who's to say? Maybe I used his blood to oil my blade, young Prince.

I won't let you *kill* anyone else in my name! I'll kill you *myself!*

Enough of this.
SMK

Don't you *touch* him.

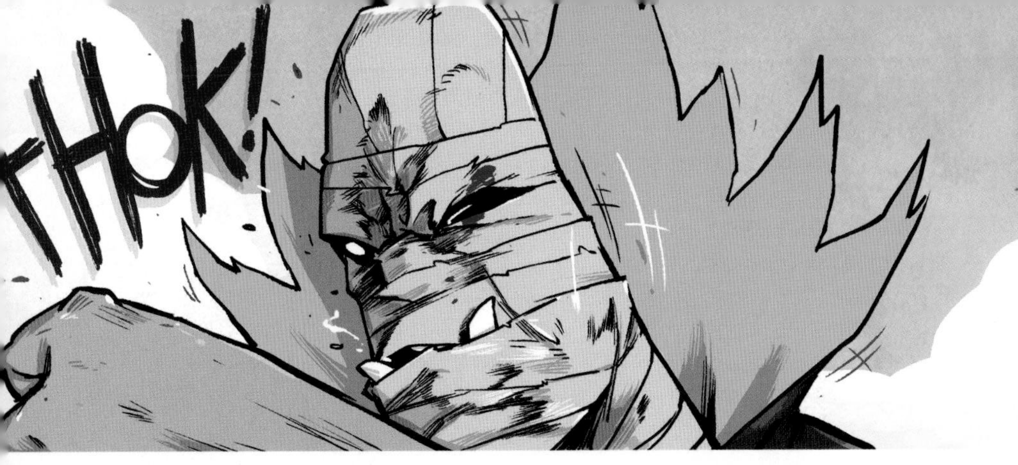
THOK!

OOF!
See, that's better. I could *feel* that.

I'm just getting started.

If he strikes me again, *remove* one of the Prince's legs.

What?

The King needs Yorik alive. Not *whole.* But you couldn't bear it, could you?

I can taste that puppy dog *love.* I could taste it on that dirty little *kitchen rat,* and I can taste it on you.
Stand down, *boy.* You've lost.

Let's go to the *cliff.* I think the young Prince needs to learn a thing or two about the *world* before he returns to Pipetown.

Where do we take them?

Come on...
Come on...

Where the heck are you little weirdos when I need you?

Creee?

Okay.
I don't know how this works...
But I need to be ***somebody*** right now. Some-body who can help my friends.

Please. Help me.

Geeebo!
Geebo!

Geeebo!
Greebo!
Geebo!

Okay...
Ah...

AAH!!

AAAHHHHHHHH!

CHAPTER SIX
THE FLIGHT

You know, I should have figured you'd be in on this, Thorn.
Your father, growing Sprytles in the back of his greenhouse...

I made him do it. It's not his fault.

And you've twisted the Prince's mind against his father. What sick creature are you?
Just take us back. Stop all this taunting.

No, your father made it clear that an example must be made.

What?
Yorik?

No! Don't you touch him! Don't you dare touch him.

How else
are you going
to learn?

I'm
sorry...I...

I...I'm not
falling.

You're not
falling.
What...

Hi.

Wow.

Yorie! **Jump** to me!

I...I don't think...
That's right, **don't think,** just jump!

Arrows!
ARROWS!!

Sir...They're coming out of the trees!
They're eating the arrows.

No. I won't allow this.

I WON'T ALLOW THIS.

Are you okay, Wynd? Can you carry both of us?

Don't see... what kinda... choice I have...

NO!

GRAB!

Ah!
Bring them down, boy. You can't carry us all...

AHHHHHH!!

Yorie. Hold onto his neck. Don't choke him.
Okay.

Let go of him!
HMF!

SSSSsss!
LET GO!

WHOOOSH!

Hold on tighter... This hurts a lot...
Okay.
I like your wings.
Thank you.

I don't understand. She should be back by now.
Someone should be back by now.

Wait, I see some-thing in the clouds...

What...

Wynd?

Prince Yorik! Thank goodness!

I'm sorry... The *Faerie General.* She died...
Lady Gwendolyn knew the risks. What matters is you're *safe,* and out of the *grasp* of Pipetown.

Wynd, what *happened* to you?
I grew *wings!*
I can *see* that!

They look so cool.
They hurt *so much.* I don't think I'm supposed to *carry* that much weight.

I wanna...
I wanna go
to sleep.

I think
we can arrange
that.
But *first*
you owe me
dinner.

Wynd...
You saved our *lives* back there... and you didn't have to. You could have gotten to the *ship* on your own with your wings.

I couldn't do that...

I *know.*
I'm sorry any of this happened to you. To *Miss Molly.* To *Lady Gwendolyn.* To all the *magic-blooded people* in Pipetown...

And I am *going* to make it up to you. I don't know how, but I *promise* you, I will!

How about...you come eat with us?

You want to **eat** with me?

I mean, it's not like we have much choice. This isn't **that** big a boat.
Oakley... He's **trying.**
Yeah, okay.

Your Highness, the Duke awaits in Northport. We're here at your command.

Then take us north.

EPILOGUE
THE DREAM

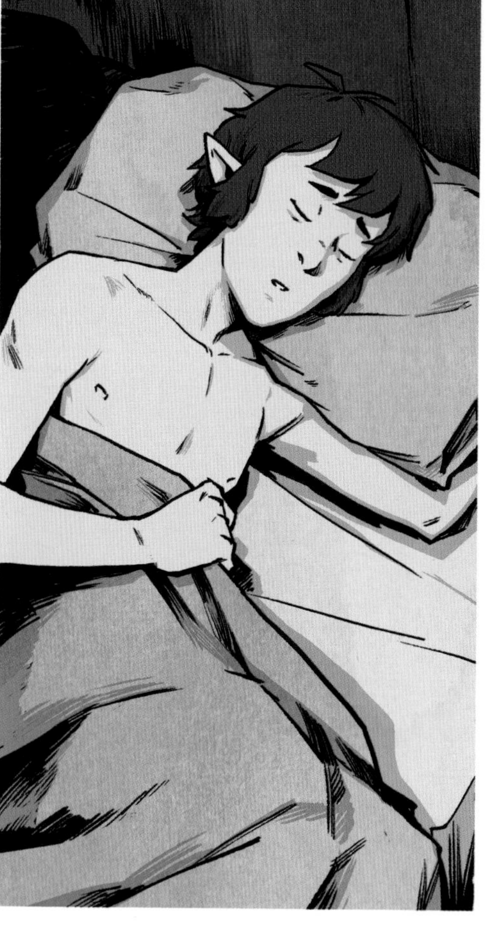

END OF
BOOK ONE

WYND

WILL RETURN IN

**BOOK TWO:
THE SECRET OF THE WINGS**

THE VINNITOY RIVER
FORT GRAYE
THE HOLD
VINNITOY PIPE CORPS.
GUARDS
WALK BY THE CANAL
FIND MOLLY
THE DARK SPOUT
THE WEIRD WOODS
STAY OUT!
STAY SAFE.
N
W
E
S

THE SALYDIAN RIVER
SALYDIAN PIPE CORPS.
THE
IMPERIAL
COURTS
PIPE CORPS.
USE EAST STAIRWELL
WATCH OUT FOR THE BANDAGED MAN!!!
IMPORT/EXPORT CENTER
GUARDS
MEET YOUR CONTACT IN SOUTH PORT!!
PIPESTREAM TO SOUTH PORT

JAMES TYNION IV is a comic book writer, best known as the writer for DC Comics' flagship series, *Batman*. In addition to the 2017 GLAAD Media Award-winning series *The Woods* with Michael Dialynas, James has also penned the critical successes *Something is Killing the Children* with Werther Dell'Edera, *Memetic*, *Cognetic*, and *Eugenic* with Eryk Donovan, *The Backstagers* with Rian Sigh, and *Ufology* with Noah J. Yuenkel and Matthew Fox from BOOM! Studios, as well as *The Department of Truth* with Martin Simmonds from Image Comics. An alumni of Sarah Lawrence College, Tynion now lives and works in New York, NY.

MICHAEL DIALYNAS is a comic artist and mini-beast wrangler that resides in Athens, Greece. He is most known for his work on the GLAAD Award-winning series *The Woods* with James Tynion IV, *Lucy Dreaming* with Max Bemis, and *Spera* from BOOM! Studios, *Teenage Mutant Ninja Turtles* from IDW, *Gotham Academy* from DC Comics, and *Amala's Blade* from Dark Horse. When he's not chained to the desk drawing comics, he tries to live a normal life and see the Earth's yellow sun every now and then. WoodenCrown.com